INDIANA JONES

and the

TEMPLE OF DOOM™

A Tale of High Adventure

INDIANA JONES

and the

TEMPLE OF DOOM™

A Tale of High Adventure

Story Adaptation by Les Martin

Random House ▙▟ New York

Based on the film
INDIANA JONES AND THE TEMPLE OF DOOM
Screenplay by Willard Huyck & Gloria Katz
Story by George Lucas

Library of Congress Cataloging in Publication Data: Martin, Les, 1934–   . Indiana Jones and the
temple of doom: a tale of high adventure. SUMMARY: While trying to recover a sacred stone belong-
ing to an Indian village, Indiana Jones and his two companions become prisoners of a ruthless sect
dedicated to the worship of the evil goddess Kali.   [1. Adventure and adventurers—Fiction]
I. Indiana Jones and the temple of doom (Motion picture) II. Title. PZ7.M36353 In
1984 [Fic] 84-1966 ISBN: 0-394-86389-5
Manufactured in the United States of America   1 2 3 4 5 6 7 8 9 0

1

The day that Short Round tried to pick Indiana Jones's pocket on a crowded Shanghai street was the luckiest day in the young Chinese boy's life.

The luck began when Indiana didn't turn Short Round over to the police. Instead he listened to Short Round's story. And when Indy heard that Short Round had lost his family in a Japanese air raid and stole only to keep from starving, Indy offered Short Round a job as local guide and general handyboy.

Even better, Indy promised to take Short Round with him to America when the daredevil archeologist wrapped up his work in China. As a head start, Indy gave Short Round a Yankee baseball cap and taught Short Round the vital American skill of driving a car.

Short Round proudly wore that baseball cap now as he sat at the wheel of a new, cream-colored 1934 Duesenberg convertible touring car in the early hours before dawn. The car was parked next to Shanghai's most

lavish nightspot, the Club Obi Wan. Indy had gone into the Obi Wan to deliver a box of ancestral ashes he had unearthed for a bigwig named Lao Che, and to collect his pay. As soon as Indy came out, they were going to drive to the airport. Thinking about the trip to America, Short Round sank back into the softly yielding leather of the driver's seat and closed his eyes. If this was a dream, he never wanted to wake up.

Loud as a pistol shot, the sound of smashing glass woke Short Round to the fact that life with Indiana Jones had one little drawback.

Sudden, violent danger.

An enormous rolling metal gong crashed through a floor-to-ceiling window on the third floor of the nightclub and bounded down the sloping tile roof. It was followed by the rolling, intertwined figures of a man and a woman. The pair tumbled to the edge of the roof and went over—into empty air.

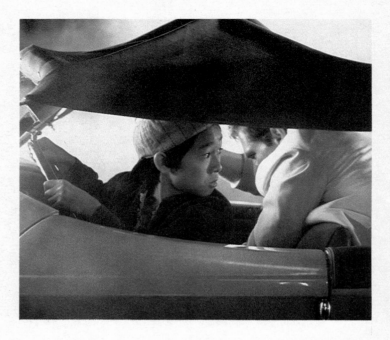

Just one thing stopped them from splattering onto the pavement.

The Duesenberg convertible.

Its leather top cushioned their fall as they went through it. And the thickly padded upholstery of the car's back seat saved them from anything worse than bruises.

Instantly Indiana Jones disengaged himself from the terrified woman still clinging to him.

"Step on it, Short Round!" he said.

"Okey-doke, Indy!" said Short Round. "Hold on to your potatoes!"

As the car shot into full speed, Short Round wondered who their female passenger was.

But right now, with a black sedan full of gunmen

already in pursuit and bullets whistling past the Duesenberg, there wasn't time to find out.

The night that Willie Scott met Indiana Jones at the
Obi Wan was the unluckiest night of the beautiful blond
singer's life. Willie saw it that way, anyway, and she
was an expert on bad luck.

Willie's singing career had bogged down in the eco-
nomic depression swamping America. Her bid to be a
big hit in the Far East had been a bust. And her plan to
find a wealthy Oriental potentate to yank her out of her
rut and put her on a solid gold pedestal had not gotten
off the ground.

That was why she had temporarily hooked up with

Lao Che. Lao called himself a merchant prince. Everyone else called him a crime lord. But whatever he was, he had enough money to keep alive Willie's dreams of a future filled with champagne and diamonds—even if he hadn't yet made them come true.

Now Indiana Jones had turned those dreams into a nightmare.

She first saw this oddball archeologist when she finished her number on the Obi Wan stage and joined Lao and his henchmen at their table. Indiana was there, squabbling about some ashes he was delivering to Lao Che, and the payment of a wad of cash and a gorgeous diamond that Lao refused to hand over.

Before Willie could beat a retreat, she was in the middle of a battle royal. The wild melee left the ashes

scattered, a Chinese friend of Indiana's dead, Indiana poisoned, the air filled with a cloud of balloons that Indiana released to screen himself from flying bullets, and the diamond knocked off the table and onto the nightclub floor.

Instantly Willie was on her hands and knees, hunting the most precious stone she had ever lusted for. She thought she saw it glinting—and grabbed what turned out to be a vial containing the antidote that could save Indiana's life.

It was then that Willie made her big mistake.

When Indiana seized a sword from the statue of a warrior to battle a thug waving a machine gun, and then slashed a cord that held a giant gong suspended, Willie grabbed that vial.

As the gong crashed down and went bounding away, Indiana grabbed her.

Struggling, they rolled after the gong, out the window, and down the sloping roof. Willie was screaming at the top of her lungs as they went over the edge and fell—where?

Dazed, Willie realized she was in the back seat of a speeding car. And a small boy wearing a baseball cap was at the wheel.

Willie was sure of only one thing in a world gone whacko.

Her luck couldn't get worse.

Willie was wrong.

As Indiana Jones gulped the antidote he had recovered from Willie and felt the burning in his gut begin to fade, he figured he had stretched his luck to the limit. Good planning had to take him the rest of the way out of this jam.

Willie, though, had different concerns.

"Look what you've done to me," she said. "My lipstick's smeared, I've broken two nails, I've got a run in my stocking—I'm a total mess!"

"If Lao gets his hands on you after you let me get that antidote, you'll find out what being a mess really means," said Indy, and he pulled out a pistol to trade shots with the black sedan hot on their trail.

Pausing to reload his weapon, he said to the driver, "Shorty! You call the airport?"

"Sure, Indy," said Short Round, not taking his eyes off the Shanghai street maze he was zooming through, scattering cars, rickshas, and pedestrians. "Got three seats—for you, me, and Wu Han."

"Wu Han's not coming," said Indy, wincing at the memory of his sidekick lying dead on the nightclub floor.

"Don't worry, Indy," said Short Round. "Short Round number one bodyguard now."

"We've got someone to use the ticket, though," said Indy.

"*Me?*" Willie protested. She heard a bullet whiz close past the window. "Me," she agreed.

She didn't change her mind again until she saw the plane that was waiting at the airport.

"No *way* I travel on a cargo plane loaded with live chickens," she said. "I'm a star. I go first class."

"Suit yourself," said Indy. He grabbed his valise and ran with Short Round to the trimotor plane. Its propellers were already spinning.

Willie took one quick look at the black sedan coming through the airport gate.

"Hey, wait up!" she shouted.

Lao Che gazed with helpless rage at the plane taking off. Then the fury on his face melted into a smile.

By the light of dawn, he could read the bold letters on the plane's body: LAO CHE AIR FREIGHT.

As Lao went to radio his orders to his plane's crew, his smile broke into a sharklike grin.

Indiana Jones and his friends had finally run out of luck.

11

At last Indy could relax. He had changed from the formal clothes he had worn into the Club Obi Wan and was back in his comfortable khaki shirt, well-worn trousers, beat-up leather jacket, and snap-brim hat. His favorite weapon, a coiled bullwhip, was hooked on a peg within easy reach. With his head braced on a crate of cackling chickens, he prepared to drop off to sleep. When he woke up, he and the others would be in Siam. From there a Pan Am clipper would take them to Los Angeles.

Indy groaned as a sound much louder than the chickens yanked him from dreamland.

It was Willie's voice.

"Indiana! The pilot's getting off the plane!"

"We there already?" said Indy groggily.

Willie's voice rose an ear-splitting notch higher.

"He's jumping! Do something!"

Indy got to his feet just in time to see the pilot and

then the co-pilot go out the plane door with parachutes on their backs. Lao Che would have been pleased to see them carrying out his orders so well.

Instantly Indy headed for the cockpit, with Willie and Short Round close behind.

"You know how to fly?" asked Willie anxiously.

"Actually, no," said Indy. "I was kind of hoping you did."

Willie made a sound that closely resembled the squawking of the chickens.

"Just kidding, sweetheart," said Indy. "I got everything under control. Altimeter—check! Stabilizer—roger! Air speed—okay! Fuel—"

There was silence as Indy said nothing—and the plane's engines went dead.

"What about the fuel?" screamed Willie.

"Uh, we've got a problem," said Indy. "They must have drained the tanks. Shorty, could you—?"

"I already check," said Short Round. "No more parachutes."

"*Look,*" gasped Willie. She was staring through the windshield—at a mountainside straight ahead.

Indy pulled desperately at the controls, and the gliding plane cleared the mountain by inches. Around them, as far as the eye could see, were snow-covered mountains with peaks swathed in clouds.

The plane tilted downward.

"We're sinking," muttered Indy.

"*Ships* sink," Willie corrected him. "Planes *crash.*"

Indy's face lit up. "That gives me an idea. Come on, Shorty!"

"What on earth do you think you're doing?" said

Willie as Indy and Short Round pulled an inflatable life raft from a plane locker and unfolded it by the open cargo door. Indy grabbed his valise and lay face down on the raft, and Short Round lay on top of him. "If you guys think I'm risking *my* life on such a nutty stunt, you're totally—"

"We're crashing!" said Indy.

"Right!" said Willie, flinging herself down on Short Round to complete a three-layer human sandwich on top of the inflating raft. Suddenly the plane hit a mountainside and the raft went flying out the door.

The raft was fully inflated by the time it hit the snow and tobaggoned out of range of the violently exploding plane.

"Indy, you the greatest!" said Short Round, holding on for dear life as they hurtled down the mountainside.

"Sometimes I amaze even myself," admitted Indy.

"I'll bet," said Willie—and then she screamed.

The raft had torn through a cluster of bushes and plummeted over a bluff into a raging river.

It wasn't until the raft reached calm waters after a long, bouncing, dipping, spinning ride on swirling, racing rapids, that Willie got back enough breath to say, "I'm totally *drenched*. Where are we, anyway?"

"That's easy," said Indy. "We're in India."

"How do you—" Willie began. Then her mouth dropped open as she followed Indy's gaze.

There, on the riverbank, stood a wizened old man wearing a tattered robe and gleaming beads.

Even more startling than the man's appearance was the expression on his face.

He looked as if he had been waiting for them to arrive.

III

The man was the shaman, the holy man, of the tiny foothill village of Mayapore. And he was indeed waiting for them to arrive.

He explained it all when they reached Mayapore—a place of desolation where starving people shuffled through their tasks like living ghosts.

"Your coming was foretold in a dream," the shaman said. "You are the answer to my prayers to Krishna. Only you can save my village from the doom devouring it."

"Sorry," said Indy. "I'm an American professor on my way home. I just need a guide to take me to Delhi."

"On the way to Delhi you will stop at the palace of Pankot," said the shaman. "You must find and destroy the evil there."

"Evil?" said Indy, with a spark of interest.

"From Pankot they came and stole the *sivalinga* from us. Since then, our crops have withered, our animals have died."

"The *sivalinga*," said Indy, leaning forward. "A sacred stone from the shrine that protects the village."

"And it is to Pankot that the evil ones have taken our children," the shaman continued.

Hearing this, Short Round suddenly realized why Mayapore was so awful. There was not a child to be seen.

Until that night.

That night a boy arrived at the village. He was little more than skin and bones. His fingers were hideously cut and bleeding. Indy himself caught the boy in his arms as the boy's last strength faded and he fell. Indy carried him into a hut and laid him on a blanket on the earthen floor.

"He was taken to Pankot," the shaman said. "He must have escaped. He is the only one who has come back to us."

The boy's eyelids fluttered as he recovered consciousness. He looked up into Indy's eyes. What he saw there made him thrust a ragged piece of cloth into Indy's hand.

"A fragment of an old manuscript," said Indy as he examined it. "A drawing of Sankara, the ancient priest who was given five stones with supreme magical powers. Powers for good—or evil."

Meanwhile, Short Round didn't have to see Indy's growing fascination with this mystery to know what Indy was going to do. The expression on Indy's face had been enough. Short Round had seen the same look when Indy rescued him from the Shanghai streets. Indy wasn't going to turn his back on kids in trouble.

Indy was going to Pankot.

25

IV

"Hey! We're going to *Delhi*!" Willie said indignantly as she stood with Indy and Short Round and looked at the palace of Pankot. Its splendor was clear even from afar.

"*You* can go to Delhi," said Indy. "Our guide is heading there to sell the village elephants. In fact, he's going there right now. He won't take us any closer to the palace—not since he saw *this*."

Indy pointed to a statue he had found in the jungle. A goddess with four arms, each one holding a human head by the hair.

"I don't blame him," said Willie, shuddering.

Willie looked at the half-naked guide, who was still jabbering excitedly in a language she didn't understand and didn't like. She looked at the elephants he was already leading away. She liked them even less.

"On second thought," she said, "where there's a palace there might be a prince. A rich prince. Maybe an unmarried prince."

"Anything's possible at Pankot," agreed Indy. Then he said, "Shorty, let's get a move on. No time to lose."

Short Round gave one last sad look of loss at the baby elephant in the herd. That playful animal was the closest thing to a pet that Short Round had ever had.

With a quick gesture, Short Round wiped a tear from his eye. He had to forget about kid stuff. He was Indy's number one bodyguard. And he had a strong hunch that Indy was going to need one in the palace of Pankot.

"It's like being in heaven," said Willie, gazing at the gold-domed Pleasure Pavilion in the palace gardens.

It was nighttime. Willie had changed into a gorgeous silk gown that had been provided by Chattar Lal, the wonderfully generous prime minister of Pankot. And she was looking forward to the feast to be served in honor of the American travelers.

The thought of food made Willie realize how famished she was. But what made her mouth really water was the idea of soon meeting the maharajah of Pankot. With this palace, he had to be filthy rich. And Chattar Lal had told her he was young. Good looking. And single.

"Now we can start getting some answers to all the questions about this place," said Indy, standing beside her.

Furnished with a respectable tweed suit from his va-

lise, Indy could actually pass for a college professor, especially since he wasn't carrying his bullwhip. Willie could even see how he might possibly be attractive, if you forgot about his rough spots.

Short Round joined them. He had been cleaned up, but his baseball cap was still perched on his head, as if defying the aristocratic surroundings. He had taken the job of carrying Indy's bullwhip.

At that moment the other guests came into the garden—wealthy merchants, nobles, court officials. With them was the prime minister, Chattar Lal, a distinguished-looking man with a smooth English university accent and the silken manners of his native Far East. He led an impeccably uniformed English officer over to Indy.

"Let me introduce Captain Blumburtt," Chattar Lal said. "He's passing through with his cavalry troops on an inspection tour. The British take such good care of their empire."

As soon as Indy could, he drew the English officer aside. "Do you know how long this palace has been reoccupied?" he asked. "I thought it had been deserted since 1830, when it was found to be headquarters for the Thuggees."

"Ah, yes, the Thuggees," said Blumburtt. "Nasty lot. Practiced human sacrifice."

"They worshipped Kali, the goddess of evil," said Indy.

"Quite so," said Blumburtt. "But that's all over. The British government wiped out the Thuggees long ago. The chaps here now are really quite a decent crew. Civilized, progressive, that sort of thing."

"But I saw a Thuggee shrine as I approached the palace," said Indy. "And the maharajah's collection of artifacts includes voodoo-like dolls, the kind that give you power over your enemies."

"All relics of the past—of historical interest only," cut in Chattar Lal, who had been standing within earshot and now joined them.

"Some of the carvings of Kali were *new*," said Indy.

"That is not possible, Dr. Jones," said Chattar Lal, his own eyes narrowing for just a split second before his face became that of a genial host once more.

A loud gong reverberated in the night air.

"I'm afraid you must save any other questions for later," said Chattar Lal. "Let us enter the pavilion. The feast is about to begin."

"I can't tell you how hungry I am," said Willie. She

sat with the throng of other guests in the Pleasure Pavilion, watching a line of servants bringing heavily laden
silver platters to the long tables.

Suddenly the servants stopped in their tracks as
Chattar Lal's booming voice announced, "His Supreme Highness, the Maharajah of Pankot."

Willie saw the other guests touching their foreheads
to the floor, and she did the same. Then she raised her
eyes and said, "Oh, *no*. Not *him*."

The maharajah was rich, dressed in sumptuous gold

and silver brocade. He was good looking, slim, and erect, without a wrinkle on his face. And he had to be single.

The maharajah was thirteen years old.

"Cheer up, Willie. Maybe he likes older women," said Indy with a grin.

"Well, at least I'll get a good meal out of this," said Willie. "I've never been so hungry in my life."

She leaned forward eagerly to inspect the silver platter that a servant had set down on the table before her.

She saw a whole roast boar, with tiny baby boars placed around it, as if it were suckling them.

"My god, sort of gruesome, isn't it?" said Willie, and motioned for a servant to bring another dish.

That turned out to be a steaming boa constrictor. With a flash of a knife, the servant slit open the huge snake to expose a mass of squirming, live eels inside.

"Come to think of it, I'm not really that hungry," Willie said, waving the platter away.

Then she stared into the soup that came next, and saw at least a dozen eyeballs floating in it.

"Looks delicious, no?" said a merchant next to her, ladling a huge portion for himself. "But you're not eating," he said to Willie in wonderment.

He motioned for another platter and grabbed a handful of shiny black baked beetles, then cracked one in half and sucked out the insides.

"I, uh, had bugs for lunch," said Willie in a shaky voice.

"Ah . . . dessert," said the merchant, licking his lips.

With a flourish, a servant set down a platter heaped with dead monkey heads. Eagerly the merchant lifted off the top of one and dipped a golden spoon inside.

"Chilled monkey brains," the merchant exulted as he brought the spoon to his mouth, then blinked in puzzlement as Willie keeled over in a dead faint.

"This is quite a meal," Indy said to Short Round as female servants helped a wobbly-kneed Willie leave the pavilion. "I wonder what our hosts are planning to serve us next."

V

When Short Round was awakened in the middle of the night, his first move was to grab the dagger he had put under his pillow. He knew right away that Indy was in trouble—and his job was to get Indy out of it.

Indy, however, had already done that job himself.

Short Round saw a huge man wearing a turban dangling from a slowly spinning overhead fan. One end of Indy's bullwhip was wrapped like a noose around his neck.

"Shorty, turn off the fan," said Indy. Then, as soon as Indy had recovered his favorite weapon, he said, "Come on, Shorty, let's get to Willie's room and make sure she's okay."

"I knew you'd show up here," said Willie when Indy burst into her room. "You men are all alike—not that I'm complaining, understand."

Willie's eyes widened as Short Round followed Indy

into the room, and her mouth opened in an unspoken question as they began to search for intruders.

Indy found nothing—nothing except a breeze coming from behind the base of a wall.

Indy's face took on the look of a hunter scenting prey. He tapped the wall and was rewarded by a hollow sound. Next he inspected a statue carved on a pillar built into the wall. Then he found what he was looking for.

Part of the statue was a lever, and when Indy pressed it, the wall swung open to become the entrance to a tunnel.

Without hesitating, Indy entered. He lit a match and read an inscription on the wall: *"Follow in the footsteps of Shiva. Do not betray his truth."* He turned to Willie and Short Round, who stood curious and frightened at the

tunnel entrance. "The same words were on the manuscript fragment that the boy who escaped from Pankot handed me. Come on, the trail is getting hot."

"Right," said Short Round, following Indy into the tunnel.

"You boys have fun in there," said Willie. "I'll see you in Delhi—because that's where I'm headed right now."

"Don't leave this room—and lock the door," said Indy.

As Indy and Short Round disappeared into the darkness of the tunnel, Willie stood frozen, suspended between her dread of staying in this weird palace and her fear of what might happen to her if she tried to flee.

But she was sure of one thing.

Into that tunnel was the last place she wanted to go.

Willie didn't want to believe her ears, but she couldn't escape the distant voice she heard.

Indy's voice, coming from deep within the tunnel.

"Willie! Get down here! I need you!"

Under different circumstances Willie might not have minded Indy saying that he needed her. But right now she looked into the dark tunnel and shuddered.

"Quick!" called Indy. "Not much more time."

Willie picked up a kerosene lamp, turned up its glow, and peered inside the tunnel.

"Ughhh," she gasped, at the same time that Indy's voice shouted desperately, "We're in trouble!"

The tunnel floor was alive with black beetles.

"I'm not really doing this—it's just a nightmare I'm

having," Willie said to herself as she heard the crunching of beetles under her slippered feet.

Her stomach felt very close to her mouth by the time she reached a large chamber and faced a locked door.

"Where are you, Indy?" she called.

"On the other side of the door," Indy answered. "It slammed shut behind us."

"Let me in," Willie said. "It's scary out here."

"It's scarier in here. We're in a room with spikes on the ceiling and floor. The spikes are closing in on us. You have to get the door open. Find the fulcrum release."

"The *what*?" said Willie.

"A *lever*. Something you *pull*. It has to be hidden somewhere—I hope."

"There're two square holes in the wall," said Willie.

"Try them—and hurry!" Indy said, his voice growing more desperate.

Gingerly Willie put her hand into the hole on the left. That one at least looked halfway clean. Her fingers groped, and found . . . nothing.

"The other one—fast!" shouted Indy.

"But it's dis*gust*ing—covered with some kind of *slime*," Willie protested.

"Reach in! The lever! The spikes are—"

"Ughhh," said Willie.

"Good work," said Indy as the door sprang open. "The spikes retracted instantly."

Willie wasn't listening. She was staring at the thick green slime that coated her arm.

Indy pulled her dazed into the room. She saw a door slowly lifting on the other side. As soon as it was high enough, Short Round went under it, eager to be out of this chamber of horrors.

"Come on," said Indy, moving toward it. By now the opening was wide enough for a howling wind to come rushing out of it.

"Wait a minute," said Willie. "Gotta get these bugs off of me."

As she reached up to brush the creepy creatures out of her hair, Indy shouted, "Look out with your elbow— don't touch that stone!"

He was too late. Willie's elbow hit the same stone that Short Round had pressed before—with the same results. The door they had entered through slammed shut, and the spikes began to emerge.

At the same time, the door on the other side of the room began to slide downward.

There was no time for words. There was barely time for Indy to grab Willie, pull her across the room, shove her through the disappearing doorway, and dive through it himself.

Indy, Short Round, and Willie stood with the closed door at their backs. In their faces was a soul-chilling wind that seemed to be blowing from the depths of the netherworld.

Willie looked into the howling darkness and shuddered.

She had a feeling that what was waiting for them ahead would make those spikes look good.

Willie's worst fears had come true.

She stood with Indy and Short Round at the other end of the tunnel, looking down at a vast underground temple dominated by a giant statue of the goddess Kali. The towering idol was adorned with carvings of corpses and severed heads. Glistening blood flowed out of her twisted mouth and down over her naked breasts. Between Kali and the immense throng of people worshipping her was a natural crevice shrouded in smoke rising from bubbling lava. More smoke rose from urns carried by chanting priests.

"It's a scene right out of hell," said Willie.

"It's a Thuggee ceremony," said Indy. "And the worst part is still to come."

On the altar, the tall high priest looked down at the writhing figure of a man tied stretched out on an iron frame. The high priest's hand swooped down—and

entered the man's chest as if the flesh were no more solid than the smoke around them. The high priest raised the man's still-beating heart high. It burst into flame, while lesser priests carried the screaming victim on the frame to the crevice. They lowered him to the molten surface of the lava, his skin blistering, his flesh smoking, his hair bursting into flame, as a sacrifice to Kali.

"Let's get out of here, *please,*" said Willie, covering her eyes.

"Quiet," said Indy, leaning forward intently as the high priest departed from the temple and the ceremony moved toward its climax.

Priests were laying three large quartz stones on the altar. The smoke curling around the altar swirled, sucked into those stones. Brought together, the three stones blazed with white fire.

"One of those stones came from Mayapore," said Indy. "The villagers knew it was magic—but they didn't know how strong the magic was. Those are the legendary Stones of Sankara. When they're brought together, the diamonds inside them glow."

"Diamonds?" said Willie, uncovering her eyes.

On the altar, the white lights seemed to glow brighter and brighter, blazing with the power to serve all humanity—or enslave it.

"Indy, I go with you," pleaded Short Round a half hour later, after the priests and worshippers had left, leaving Kali alone to gaze down at the blazing stones.

"Sorry, Shorty, but some things I have to do by myself," said Indy. "Besides, you have to stay here with Willie and protect her. No telling who might be around here."

"Someday you're going to get killed," said Willie.

"Not today," said Indy. He took his bullwhip and shoulder bag from Short Round. "See you later."

The descent from the tunnel mouth to the temple was difficult but not impossible. After Indy shimmied down a huge temple column, using carved stone cobras and lions as footrests, only the wide crevice with its bubbling lava separated him from Kali's altar.

His bullwhip hissed through the air. It wrapped around the trunk of a giant elephant statue on the other side. And Indy swung over the lava to land within reach of his goal.

He looked up and saw Kali's face glowering down at him, as if she were enraged at this sacrilege.

He looked down at the stones, and in spite of himself he felt a tremor of fear at the thought of coming in contact with their awesome force.

Then he thought of the desolate village from which one of the stones had been stolen, and one by one he picked them up and dropped them into his sack.

Suddenly he froze.

From behind Kali came a sound. An echoing, moaning sound. Indy was afraid he knew what it was. The sound of many distant voices, all sharing the same despair.

Behind Kali he found a passageway. Moving into it, he saw a glow of light in the darkness ahead. That light beamed upward from an enormous pit. At its edge, Indy gazed down at a scene that first made him sick, then filled him with rage.

The bottom of the pit was a bee's hive of activity— endless streams of skeleton-thin figures crawling in and out of narrow tunnels, dragging sacks of dirt and rock, while heavily armed guards prodded them along. Those figures were children, or what was left of them.

When Indy saw a guard savagely beating a kid who had collapsed with exhaustion, he could watch no longer. He picked up a large rock and hurled it downward— only to see with shock that the guard simply reached up and caught it in one huge hand.

Then came an even bigger shock.

Another huge hand gripped his shoulder and turned him around.

Indy was surrounded by huge armed guards—and there was no escaping their brutal fury.

VI

The first thing Indy saw when he opened his eyes was Short Round's face. He had a brief hope that the whole thing had been a bad dream. Then he saw that Short Round was in chains. When he tried to come to Short Round's aid, he realized he was in chains, too, in a dimly lit cell.

"Thuggees spot me and Willie," said Short Round. "I fight good, but they get me. Willie get away, though. Maybe she bring help, huh, Indy?"

"Maybe," said Indy. "I think she's tougher than she acts." Then he noticed that they weren't alone. A ragged figure crouched in the corner. "Who's your friend?"

"This is Nainsukh—one of the kids they take from the village," said Short Round. "He work in mines."

"We children only ones small enough to crawl in tunnels," said Nainsukh. "But now I am too big for that."

"What they do to you now?" asked Short Round.

"I pray to Shiva they kill me," said Nainsukh. "But they will not. They will make me drink blood of Kali. Then I fall into black sleep of Kali. I be Kali's slave."

Indy was about to ask more about the blood of Kali when the cell door swung open. Two massively muscled guards and a priest of Kali came to take Indy and Short Round to the man who could answer all questions about the goddess of death and destruction.

The high priest, Mola Ram, stood in his chamber before a statue of Kali even more hideous than the temple idol. The severed heads adorning her were not carved of stone—they were real. The blood dripping from her mouth was fresh. The sacred stones seemed to glow even more brightly on her altar.

"You were caught stealing the Sankara Stones," Mola Ram said, glaring at Indy and Short Round.

"Nobody's perfect," said Indy, shrugging. "Anyway, you stole at least one of them yourself."

"All of them belong to Kali," Mola Ram said. "There were five stones in the beginning. Already we have these three. And we know that the other two are buried somewhere beneath the palace. They were hidden there by loyal priests when the British raided Pankot almost a hundred years ago."

"That's what you've got those kids, those *slaves*, digging for?" said Indy, his muscles taut with anger. How he wished he had his bullwhip in his hand now.

"Soon we will possess all five stones—and Kali will possess all the world," said Mola Ram, drawing his tall, robed body up to its full height.

"You've got quite a line there," said Indy. "I can see

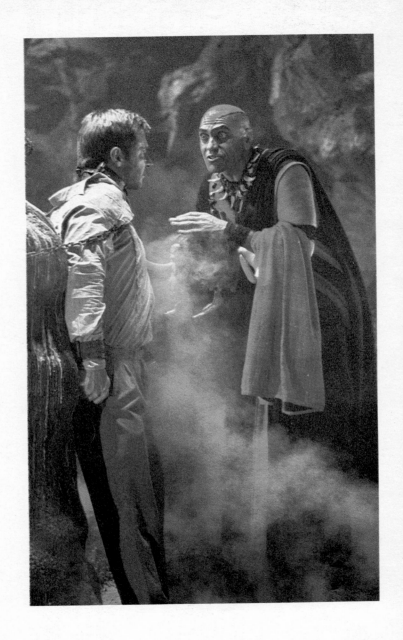

why you're such a big hit with your congregation."

"You don't believe me?" said Mola Ram. "You will, Dr. Jones." He smiled. "You will become a true believer."

Suddenly Mola Ram bowed down. The maharajah was entering the room.

"Your Highness will witness the conversion of this unbeliever," said Mola Ram, and nodded to the guards.

Short Round was held struggling helplessly while two guards tied Indy to a rock. A boy came through the door carrying a human skull, and Short Round stiffened. It was Nainsukh. But *this* Nainsukh wore robes instead of rags, and he moved like a sleepwalker.

The maharajah stood before Indy. "You will not suffer," he said. "*I* recently came of age and tasted the blood of Kali."

Mola Ram took the skull filled with blood and tilted it toward Indy's lips as the guards forced Indy's jaws apart.

The blood flowed into Indy's mouth—and shot out again as he spat full force.

The maharajah sprang back, his royal garb blood-splattered. From his pocket he took a small clay statue—a crude likeness of Indiana Jones.

"I will teach you to obey," the maharajah snarled, and thrust the statue into a flaming urn.

Indy screamed as if his flesh were on fire.

The maharajah withdrew the statue, and Indiana sank back in relief. But the maharajah was not finished.

He picked up Indy's bullwhip, which had been brought in by the guards. Expertly he cracked it in the air—and Short Round could not keep from crying out when its

lash tore into his shoulder. Then it was Indy's turn. The lash tore through his shirt, and lines of blood appeared on his skin as if drawn with a dripping brush.

"The blood of Kali will taste better to you now," the maharajah said.

"No, no!" shouted Short Round as he watched the skull tilting once more toward Indy's lips.

VII

Indy came out of the tunnel and into Willie's room. He found her there with Chattar Lal and Captain Blumburtt.

Her eyes shone with joy when she saw him. She did not notice his eyes—the lifeless eyes of a sleepwalking slave of Kali.

"Tell the prime minister and the captain that I'm not crazy, Indy," she pleaded. "Tell them about the underground temple. Tell them about the human sacrifice. Tell them they have to destroy that temple and then find Shorty and save him."

Indy gently enfolded her in his arms.

"It's okay, baby," he said. "You're all right now."

Ever so gently he laid her down on her bed.

"Take a little nap," he said, his voice soothing, almost hypnotic. "I'll take care of everything."

"I know you will, Indy. . . . I know I can . . . count on . . ." Willie murmured as she dropped into a dreamless sleep, happy at last to be in strong hands, safe after so endless a nightmare.

Indy turned to Chattar Lal and the English officer.

"Poor kid," he said. "She's had a rough time these past couple of days. When she ran into a bunch of bugs in the tunnel, it must have been the last straw. She passed out cold. I carried her back here to sleep it off. She must have had nightmares."

"The poor child," said Chattar Lal, with great sympathy.

"So there's nothing there?" said Blumburtt.

"Just a dead end," said Indy.

"Well, then, that winds up my visit here," the captain said. "My troops are already saddled up and ready to leave. My report will note that we found nothing unusual here in Pankot."

"The maharajah will be pleased," said Chattar Lal, bowing in a show of humble gratitude.

Blumburtt turned to Indy. "Needless to say, Dr. Jones, we'd be happy to escort you and the lady to Delhi."

"Thank you," said Indy as his eyes met Chattar Lal's, "but I don't think Willie is ready to travel yet."

The trip that Chattar Lal planned for Willie was a short one—to the underground temple.

Both Chattar Lal and the high priest, Mola Ram, were delighted to see how readily Indy obeyed orders, carrying Willie to the altar himself. Kali clearly had a most willing and able new servant.

By now Willie was fully awake to the horror of what had happened to Indy and the even greater horror of what was about to happen to her.

The statue of Kali towered above her as she writhed on the iron frame on the temple altar. Loud in her ears was the chanting of Mola Ram. Vivid in her memory was the human sacrifice she had spied from the tunnel mouth such a short but distant time before.

Indy stood beside the iron frame, looking at her with eyes that seemed a million miles away. Desperately she tried to reach him with her voice.

"Please, don't let them do this. Help me, Indy!"

She looked with frantic hope into Indy's eyes and saw . . . nothing.

"There must be a way to wake you up!" she cried. "There must be!"

Short Round knew how to wake Indy up.

He learned the secret from a guard who was flaying him with a strap to teach him the rules of working in the mines with the other slave children. An accidental spray of molten lava from a fissure in the mine wall seared the guard's leg. The guard screamed—then stood bewildered, as if not knowing what he was doing there with the strap in his hand. Other guards led the man away—but not before Short Round had seen life returning to fill the emptiness of the man's eyes.

Pain, thought Short Round. *Pain of fire wake the guard from the sleep of Kali. Pain of fire wake Indy, too. Must get to Indy. Wake him. Save him.*

Short Round knew of only one way to accomplish this impossible task. He had to think of what Indy would do now.

Taking advantage of the guard's absence, he used a rock to smash the chains that bound him. Then he spotted a ladder leading from the mine pit floor to a tunnel high on its wall, and scurried up it.

Putting his finger to his lips to warn the startled kid working in the tunnel to be silent, he pushed the ladder away from the wall.

Balanced on the top rung as the ladder arced across the pit, Short Round braced his legs to make a do-or-die leap for freedom.

His freedom—and Indy's.

Pain.

Indy felt it shooting through every fiber of his body. Then he saw Short Round standing with the flaming torch that had scorched his skin.

"What the—?" Indy began, then saw that there was no time for questions.

Next to the temple crevice, priests were lowering a screaming Willie stretched out on an iron frame toward the lava. Other priests were racing to capture Short Round as Mola Ram shouted orders. Chattar Lal had leaped up onto the altar with a drawn dagger.

"Don't worry, Shorty, I'm okay now," Indy said under his breath to Short Round. He lifted the boy high over his head, as if preparing to toss him into the lava.

Mola Ram smiled. Chattar Lal lowered his dagger. The charging priests came to a halt. And Indy had the breathing space he needed to swing into action.

With no wasted motion, he set Short Round down on the crevice edge, smashed aside the priests lowering Willie to her doom, and feverishly cranked the iron frame upward.

An evil light flared in Chattar Lal's eyes as he moved to stop this sacrilege. He almost succeeded. He was sawing through the rope pulling Willie to safety when Indy kicked the dagger from his hand. His last fierce defense of Kali was a rush at Indy—a rush that sent him shrieking over the crevice edge.

Indy was too busy to watch him hit the lava. With Short Round and Willie following, Indy battered his

way to where Mola Ram stood over the Sankara Stones. A moment later Mola Ram was flat on his back, the stones were in Indy's shoulder bag, and Indy and his friends had disappeared into the entrance leading to the mines.

Mola Ram stumbled to his feet, holding his jaw.

"You fool!" he roared after the vanished Indy. "You will never escape!"

VIII

I ndy and his friends were devils in disguise.
Mola Ram was sure of that, after hearing what
the fleeing unbelievers had done.

They had freed the children in the mine, with Indy
knocking out guards as if they were straw men.

They had awakened the maharajah from the sleep of
Kali the same way Short Round had awakened Indy,
after the maharajah had almost put Indy out of action
by sticking pins into the clay statue of him.

They had found their way through the maze of tunnels beneath the palace, the maharajah guiding them
before leaving to seek assistance from the outside world.

They had survived a giant pile-up of racing mine cars
and a huge flood of underground water—the same
crash and torrent that had wiped out many of the fierc-
est Thuggee fighting men and killer priests.

But now they would go no farther. At last Mola Ram had Indy and his friends within his grasp.

Willie and Short Round had been caught as they crossed the narrow, swaying rope bridge over the deep gorge that lay between them and freedom. They had not expected to find Mola Ram and his men at the other end, blocking their way. Now they were held struggling in Thuggee hands as Indy paused in the middle of the bridge. He looked back to see Thuggees coming at him from that direction too. He looked down and saw the snouts of crocodiles breaking the surface of churning water hundreds of feet below.

"You're trapped!" shouted Mola Ram. "Give up!"

"I've got a better idea," Indy called back. "Call off your men. And let my friends go!"

"You're not in a position to give orders," said Mola Ram, and gestured for his men to close in.

"If you want your precious stones, do what I say," said Indy, holding up the shoulder bag containing the Sankara Stones. To show what he meant, he started to sever a rope bridge span with a stolen Thuggee sword.

"You will not commit suicide just to save those stones," said Mola Ram.

"How much you want to bet?" said Indy as he cut through one span and raised his sword to the other.

"Then your friends will die with you!" And Mola Ram shoved Short Round and Willie back onto the bridge.

The high priest smiled as he and his men followed on their heels and headed toward Indy. Indy might have sacrificed himself, but Mola Ram knew he would not sacrifice his friends. Indy might be a devil, but he was a foreign devil, corrupted by pity and kindness, too soft to stand up to the ruthless strength of Kali.

Short Round knew better. He grabbed tight hold of the rope of the bridge and with his eyes told Willie to do the same—just before the bridge fell apart under the last vicious swipe of Indy's sword.

The screams of falling Thuggees echoed in the gorge as Short Round and Willie climbed hand over hand on the dangling rope to safety.

There was no safety for Indy, though. Mola Ram was clinging to the rope above him. His feet were smashing at Indy's head. Then the priest's hand darted down like lightning to grab Indy's shoulder bag as Indy fell.

Watching from above, Short Round and Willie clung together in horror—then relaxed as Indy caught hold of the last inches of rope and started upward after the fleeing Mola Ram.

"Must help Indy," said Short Round, and began to throw stones at Mola Ram's head.

But Mola Ram had help too. Hundreds of arrows streamed through the air from Thuggee archers across the gorge. They hit the bridge, and they came very close to hitting Indy as he climbed.

"Willie, look!" said Short Round, pointing to a swarm of British cavalry charging toward the archers.

"The maharajah must have reached Captain Blumburtt," said Willie.

"Maharajah okay kid," said Short Round. "Now only Mola Ram guy left. Indy take care of him."

Indy was not so sure of that.

Mola Ram's hand was reaching for his chest—to plunge in and seize his heart. Those evil, enchanted fingers were entering him already, and desperately Indy seized Mola Ram's wrist.

Inch by inch Indy forced the hand away, then grabbed for the bag containing the Sankara Stones.

"Those stones are mine!" screamed Mola Ram, clutching the bag with inhuman strength.

"No," said Indy. "You've violated Sankara's divine command." And in the Sanskrit language of the ancients, Indy pronounced Sankara's holy words: "Follow in the footsteps of Shiva. *Do not betray his truth.*"

Before Mola Ram's startled eyes, the bag in his hand began to glow, then burn. Through the flaming fabric the sacred stones spilled into the empty air. Frantically the high priest of Kali reached for them as they fell, and as the hideous, searing agony of touching them loosened his grip on the dangling bridge, the evil light in his eyes died.

His face was the face of a man awakened from a nightmare as he fell to the raging waters and ravenous crocodiles below.

"I guess Mola Ram got what he wanted, anyway— to keep those stones to the end," said Willie, looking down at where the high priest and the stones had disappeared.

"Not quite," said Indy, standing beside her.

He reached into his pocket and pulled out what he had dared to catch as it fell—sure that it would do evil only to those with evil in them.

The last Sankara Stone.

IX

"I figured you would keep that stone for yourself. I mean, all that fortune and glory is right up your alley," Willie said to Indy as they approached Mayapore. She and Indy and Short Round were accompanied by the throng of village children coming home, and the joyous light in the children's eyes matched the holy light of the sacred stone in Indy's hand.

"It'll do more good here than in some museum," said Indy. "Besides, who knows what other goodies we can find between here and Delhi?"

"What do you mean, *we*?" said Willie. "If you think I'm risking my career—not to mention my life—on any more crazy adventures, you're even more nuts than I think you are." She turned from him and headed toward the assembled villagers. "Hey, anyone here to take me to Delhi? I'm pretty good on an elephant, though I'd prefer a taxi . . ."

Something wrapped itself around her waist—some-

thing very much like a snake. She opened her mouth to scream—then realized what it was.

Indy's bullwhip, pulling her back to him.

Then Indy's arms were around her, and suddenly she didn't feel like screaming at all.

Short Round wasn't concerned with this grownup foolishness. He was watching something far more important.

The village elephant herdsman was leading back the animals he hadn't been able to sell.

The eyes of the baby elephant at the end of the line lit up when they met Short Round's suddenly shining eyes. The baby elephant quickened its pace to meet Short Round as the boy ran to his beloved pet.

With his arms wrapped as far as they could go around the baby elephant's neck, Short Round had to think this was the luckiest day of his life.

The second luckiest, anyway, he thought, as he remembered the day he had met Indiana Jones.